SHINO AND THE CHAOS CREW

The Day of the GALLOPING GARGOYLES

Written by Chris Callaghan and Zoë Clarke

Illustrated by Amit Tayal

Collins

Shinoy and the Chaos Crew

When Shinoy downloads the Chaos Crew app on his phone, a glitch in the system gives him the power to summon his TV heroes into his world.

With the team on board, Shinoy can figure out what dastardly plans the red-eyed S.N.A.I.R., a Super Nasty Artificial Intelligent Robot, has come up with, and save the day.

Shinoy and Myra were standing in front of the old schoolhouse.

"According to the guidebook, it's built in the Gothic style," Shinoy yawned. "What does that mean?"

"Lots of arches and stained-glass windows," said Myra. "I thought you'd like the gargoyles."

Shinoy was researching old buildings for a History project. He looked up at the roof of the old schoolhouse. A row of hideous creatures carved from stone leered down at them. The gargoyles had wings and horns and sharp teeth. Now they *were* interesting.

3

"What's that noise?" Myra asked.

Shinoy listened. There was a faint grating sound.

Myra looked at Shinoy and said,
"That gargoyle's moved!"

Shinoy looked at Myra. "Gargoyles are *stone*.
They don't move." He swiped through
the photographs he'd just taken. Then he looked
back at the roof. The gargoyle *had* moved.

4

"You're going to call the Catastrophe Crew, aren't you?" Myra groaned.

Shinoy grinned. "Call to Action, Chaos Crew!"

Shinoy activated the Chaos Crew app on his phone. There was a

Nothing happened.

Shinoy pressed the app button again. This time, there was a flash of light and Mustang Harry, Chaos Crew warrior dog, appeared.

"Greetings, friends –"
Harry began.

There was a loud *CRACK* and another flash of light. Super-sneaky Lazlo landed heavily on top of Harry.

Myra sniggered.
"Two for one!"

Harry squeezed out from under Lazlo.
"I arrived 0.025 seconds before you.
This is clearly my mission."

"I was about to have lunch," grumbled Lazlo.
"You can have this mission!"

"Maybe, we need *both* of you," Shinoy said.

"We've got a gargoyle problem," Shinoy explained.

Lazlo dusted himself off. "A what now?"

Shinoy pointed at the roof and Myra showed them the photos.

"They're not moving now," Lazlo observed.

"One's actually missing," Shinoy said, nodding at an empty plinth.

Harry sniffed the ground. "There's a stone deposit here. I'm just analysing it ... It's granite."

"That's what the guidebook says these gargoyles are made of," Shinoy confirmed.

Suddenly Harry's ears went up. "I've found a trail. Follow me!" He bounded away from the old schoolhouse at high speed.

10.5 minutes later (according to Harry), the trail led them to the library. They hid behind a pillar near the door.

There was a large gargoyle, guarding the doorway. Hopping up and down in front of it was a small gargoyle. It looked very cross.

"Wake up, you stone lump! Wake up, wake UP!"

"Do gargoyles usually talk?" Lazlo whispered.

"No!" Shinoy and Myra said together.

There was a low, grating sound. The large gargoyle slowly turned its head.

"Ooh, Crag! Look at your grumpy face!" squeaked the small gargoyle.

"You'd be grumpy too, Gorge, stuck out in the rain for hundreds of years. You're an under-roof gargoyle. A decorative pet, really."

"Hark at you!" Gorge gnashed its teeth. "I direct water away from *my* building!"

Crag glowered. "And I protect my building and ward off undesirables. Sadly, not you."

"Well, someone give you the Gargoyle of the Year prize! I've come to fetch you. Grampian and Cairn are in grave danger!"

Crag flexed its back. Stone wings cracked as they opened. Grabbing Gorge in its clawed feet, Crag rose into the air and flew off.

"That was weird," Shinoy said.

"They're heading west," Harry barked.

Lazlo started running. "I'll sneak ahead!"

Gargoyles from other buildings prised themselves from roofs and hurtled after Crag and Gorge.

"There's a large building coming up in 26 seconds. Something called a bank," said Harry.

"It's not there any more," Shinoy said.

They skidded to a halt in front of a building site, where there was a large advertising board.

"Red Eye?" Myra said.

Shinoy looked at Harry. "S.N.A.I.R.!"

Harry sniffed. "There's a concentration of granite nearby. Where's Lazlo?"

They found Lazlo surrounded by gargoyles.

"Told you others would come." Gorge looked smug. "Saw them when I was getting Crag, I did."

"How are you alive?" Myra asked the gargoyles. "*Why* are you alive?"

Crag peered at her closely. "We were *always* alive. We choose to keep our stone form."

"So who are Grampian and Cairn and why are they in danger?"

Shinoy looked at the broken arches. "Grampian and Cairn are *gargoyles*!" he said. "I'm right, aren't I? They were on the bank."

"We're on a rescue mission but we may be too late!" Gorge sniffed. "They're the oldest gargoyles in Flat Hill."

Harry sniffed. "No granite readings on the building site."

Gorge hopped up and down. "They're made of soft limestone, not hard granite like me and Crag."

Harry checked again. "There's a limestone reading under those bricks."

The gargoyles galloped over and started picking bricks off with their claws. As the bricks fell away, they could see two weathered gargoyles.

Shinoy and Myra lifted them out carefully.

Gorge whispered, "Grampian ... Cairn ... we've come to save you."

An eye opened, and then another.

"Ha! Took your time!" Grampian said.

Cairn smiled. "You great granite grannies!"

"We need somewhere safe for them," Shinoy said.

"Library?" Myra suggested. "We can put them on the shelves like bookends."

"Crag can look out for them," Shinoy agreed.

Gorge grinned. "We like that idea!"

Some time later ...

"Mission accomplished," Harry said. "I think it went well. Apart from Lazlo being captured by gargoyles."

Lazlo huffed.

"Now all I have to do is my History project," Shinoy said.

"We can tell you all about gargoyles," Gorge offered. "Just don't mention the talking bit ..."

The Flat Hill gargoyles

23

Ideas for reading

Written by Clare Dowdall, PhD
Lecturer and Primary Literacy Consultant

Reading objectives

- discuss the sequence of events in books and how items of information are related
- discuss and clarify the meanings of words, linking new meanings to known vocabulary
- draw on what they already know or on background information and vocabulary provided by the teacher
- predict what might happen on the basis of what has been read so far

Spoken language objectives

- use relevant strategies to build their vocabulary
- speak audibly and fluently with an increasing command of spoken English
- participate in discussions, presentations, performances and debates

Curriculum links: History – significant places; Art and Design – use materials to work creatively

Word count: 969

Interest words: galloping, gargoyles, demolished, Gothic, hideous, leered, plinth, deposit, granite, under-roof, decorative, gnashed, glowered, undesirables, flexed, prised, limestone, weathered

Resources: whiteboards and pens, paper and pencils, modelling clay, ICT for research, digital cameras to photograph gargoyles

Build a context for reading

- Look at the front cover and read the title. Talk about what gargoyles are, and ask children about any experiences of seeing them.
- Look closely at the gargoyles in the image on the front cover. Make a list of adjectives and noun phrases to describe the gargoyles, e.g. stony body, sharp teeth, mean eyes …
- Read the blurb. Check that children know what *demolished* means. Challenge children to predict why the stone gargoyles have come to life, and what they're up to. Who do they think the surprise visitor may be?